LISTEN DIDI...

PUTUL MANGNI MANDAL

ISBN 979-888555826-6

To all the women living in the negligible lanes of some mohalla. You will not be forgotten.

Contents

Foreword

Putul Mangni Mandal exhibits extraordinary talent in commemorating ordinary people and their narratives in a beautiful and engaging fashion. Her writings hold truth and benign upon the roots. The beauty of her work lies in the simplicity in which these stories have been written. She presents to you the 'raw truth'. She does not furbish her language or stories to make them more adaptable to the likes of the readers. Rather she writes what she wants the readers to read, for the readers to know, and for them to acknowledge. Her work isn't restrained by boundaries and margins as she voices the plight of the marginalized.

I met Pooja Rai on academic grounds. We both were pursuing our Master's degree program in English Literature from the same institution. Though we could only have offline engagements with our coursework for about a semester only, we got to connect on many levels. After we completed our Master's program, we continued to be acquainted. I read some of her poetries that she had shared and all I saw was potential. She has a comprehensive soul, which when put into words could create nothing less than beauty. She took an Academic writing course that I was teaching at that time and that got us talking in depth about our lives and aspirations. When I started the Academic and Creative Writing Training Internship program in my company (Nrityangana Kala Kendra), I couldn't let go of the opportunity to work with her. In the twelve weeks that we worked together, Pooja wrote some beautiful pieces; some of which have already been published. In fact, the book that you hold in your hands is the product of an individually assigned creative writing project that she worked on during the internship. She continues to work as a freelance writer for the company and keeps surprising me with her talents.

I can honestly say that I feel she has a really bright future and she is going to have many more gigantic achievements in her life. She has been a really good friend and has taught me a lot as well during all this while. I am extremely proud of her for how far she has come and how much growth she has bestowed upon herself in the little time we had.

Her writings are a breath of fresh air produced in the capital of our country where the AQI hasn't dropped below 200 in quite some time. Her stories deal with serious issues and portray them sometimes as a mere truth and at other moments as touches of sarcasm. She writes about how women are treated by society in general, by men, and by other women.

She brings light to molestation in her fourth story through Nargis. A child is molested and is told by her mother that it was nothing and she shouldn't mention the incident to anyone. Ishita's uncle-in-law had been abusing her. The solution to the issue was sought to be to get the girl married to a complete stranger and perhaps even without her consent. As she runs away from the house of her in-laws, the family of her boyfriend does not accept her as they belong to the 'supposed' higher class of the society and she does not. The very idea that it's still tolerable for the man to sleep around but forbidden for a woman to love another has been established in the first story itself.

Where Imarati questions the integrity of Kajal's mother-in-law to be unfair to her daughter, she forgets that she herself has been judging and putting Ishita under scrutiny without understanding her plight. What Kajal faces at the hands of her in-laws is something that is still prevalent in many parts of the country. Women are thought to be only fit to do the household chores along with bearing and taking care of children.

A girl should learn all household chores. She should serve the food for everyone but a boy shouldn't even get his own food. Pooja Rai writes as her alias, Putul Mangni Mandal. She questions- why this disparity? Why should one be objected to such distinctions based on gender, something that is what we are born with? What gives men the privilege to demand more privileges?

"Listen Didi..." is an amazing start for Putul Mangni Mandal and a treat for her readers. I'd highly recommend everyone to read this novella and appreciate its nonchalance. These stories make you think, assess and evaluate on your own the state of the marginalized women.

Swarnika

Director-Mentor
Nrityangana Kala Kendra

Acknowledgements

I would like to acknowledge a great debt that I bear to Nrityangana Kala Kendra and especially my good friend Swarnika who happens to be the director of this company. It was her consistent appreciation, encouragement, and kindness that helped me become more confident and competent.

I am also grateful to another good friend of mine Deepanshi Ailawadi whose constructive analysis of my works and honest reviews helped me locate them and improve where needed.

Dare not to leave a very important person behind, I would like to convey not thanks but my love to the dearest and closest friend of mine, Pratibha (Sahu). She does not understand literature very much but her confident belief in me has contributed significantly to my overall creative makeup.

And at last but not even near to the least, I would like to express my gratitude to the supreme power which has endowed me with such great parents. Although it is only the beginning of a long journey, without their unyielding belief in me and unconditional support, It would have been enormously difficult to build myself up to the person I am today.

Thanks and love to all.

Prologue

In the cardiac network of vibrant bungalows in a posh society named Vilaasniketan, a weary cluster of grey houses is stuck to an abandoned edge like unpleasant fat sticks to the walls of the artery. And the weary people residing in its weary lanes often find their livelihood at the golden doorsteps of Vilaasniketan's Olympians bungalows by which this place is recognised from even a good distance. One is a cook, one is probably a driver, one is going to be a guard and another is a gardener or maybe a cleaner. The turgidity of the place depends so much on the haggard hands of these negligible people that the topic to demolish their wiggling tents they call home, is never held up into the limelight and this wry cluster becomes a temporarily permanent colony of servants. It has been so for about thirty six years now, but this colony still looks as old as when it was new and beneath the tin shelters of this colony, a circle of women is revolving like Pluto — unrecognised and forlorn. But unlike Pluto, they are not alone. They have companions to convey their sorrow to. They admiringly call them Didi who by the chance of living in the almost same conditions, can feel the pain of wearing torned shoes. Let us eardrop some of these chats and peep through some windows to understand some of their stories but beware there is rarely a chance to hear them from horse's mouth. Still, let us try to become a Didi.

CHAPTER ONE

A ceremonial crowd has gathered around a government water tanker on a road outside the colony. Most of them are women and small children. Everyone is holding pails and cans as many as the hooks of ten fingers can hold. A few are busy pushing others away by hand and by mouth if they have to, around the ejaculating stream of piped water. A few are teenagers among them. Rebellious as their nature is, they have managed to climb atop the tanker and insert pipes to fill their canes by themselves. The driver of the lorry is smoking at a distance, away from all this chaos.

A woman in a black petticoat and sheer pink blouse is sitting on the upside bottom of a pail. She is pumping a few puffs of bidi on and off to light it properly as she waits for her turn in the queue to the ejaculate water. Fifty has not gone anywhere if one considers her age. But why would one? People fear her. She is like a boss around here.

"Aye, you'll fill only this can. Right? The next will be my turn. The doctor has advised me not to sit for long like this. I have back pain issues."

"Alright, Imarati didi...", says a woman whose last can is about to be filled.

A young woman in a small, lean figure is penetrating through the loose crowd. The left side of her face is partially covered with a black scarf which is tucked between her teeth while the bright red lips spark remarkably on her pale face. The ample space in her salwar is filled with air as she steps the right foot forward and withdraws quickly with the pace of the forwarding next step. Although her hair is tied tightly in a bun, a few sturdy locks are still writhing on her temple. She is carrying a red plastic bucket in one hand which has a yellow saffola can of 5ltrs fitted closely inside it. If one is eager enough to narrow one's eyes to look closely, one can find salty white lines of rolled drops over the bucket.

"Listen didi, please fill this bucket. I need to be somewhere urgently", she asks Imarati with a puckered forehead.

" Where to? Tell me first" says Imarati with a grim face.

"My lady-boss of Vilaasniketan has an engagement party today and I am needed urgently." She goes on. The wrinkles are still lined up.

"So?" Imrati shoots like an arrow.

"It's only today. Didi! I won't ask again, I swear your head!"

"So that I die quickly and you will be spared a few buckets? Don't you dare swear on my life, I have two grandkids to look after? I still have not lived a life of leisure", Imarati flushed out.

"Arey, nah nah Didi, may my age be added to yours," she says amicably.

A smile flits across Imarati's face but she composes her emotions and replies with a firm face, " and what'd you suggest? should I scrap corn in that unnecessarily long life? You're still very young Ashik's mommy. You ought to have a long life." And she carefully gives her way to the water tap.

Ashik's mother hastily places her pail down the streaming water. "Achha... tell me one thing. What would your boss say about the Blue Moon shining on your dry face?".

Ashik's mother hesitatingly tries to veil a bruise aligning the rim of the socket of her left eye." Didi, my boss, knows about him. She even gets worried when I tell her that my man beats me."

"What else would she do after all? It is your parents' fault."

No didi, they are poor folks and you tell me, aren't five daughters such a big burden on a father's shoulder? One can't expect all five fingers even. I have to compromise, especially when he can't even take care of himself. The doctor tells him not to drink otherwise the situation would get worse but he doesn't care a bit. What do you say?" She says as she lifts her bucket which is now vomiting water.

"What you say is true indeed", says Imarati, placing her can down at the same spot. Ashik's mother lifts her bucket onto her head, grips tightly onto the ears of the can, and bends towards her house down the gully.

A tall woman who had her entire face all covered behind the veil was holding her breath but now, seeing Ashik's mother's back, she bursts out finally in an irritatingly sharp voice, " *Pran chhoot jaayen par vishwasundari ki lipastik na chhootey* (one can lose life but never a lipstick)... My son Ramu was telling me that her man was drunk to the tips of fingers yesterday."

"Tsk-tsk-tsk... God knows why men drink that bitter piss", Imarati says wryly.

The lady blurts out, "listen to what happened next didi... so her man comes and asks her to make an omelette and she does. Then he tells her to go to bed while he heads out. But she doesn't sleep. Instead, she stands across the door blocking it with her both arms. It makes him furious and he starts beating her blue", she goes on.

Imarati looks very surprised. "But why on earth would she do such a thing? She perfectly knows how aggressive he becomes after a quarter of cheap liquor."

"Exactly! The matter was something else."

"What do you mean?"

"He was meaning to meet Jyoti's mother in that late hour."

"But why? Why would he go to his elder brother's wife."

"How silly of you Imarati didi. Every piece of information concerning every event that takes place in our gully reaches you first, yet you don't know about such a scandalous thing?"

"Out with it, will you!"

The lady leans towards Imarti and whispers, "Ashik's father has a connection with Jyoti's mother."

"What kind of connection?"

"Oho Didi, that dirty connection. He keeps her to himself. You get it?"

"Hmmm... Now it's all making sense... but I had heard that it was Ashik's mother who was in connection with some boy at work?"

"Exactly, now you're back on track. That too is true. I have seen her by these very eyes of mine with that boy walking hand in hand."

"Where?...Hand in hand! In that case, there must be a connection."

"There is! Isn't that what I'm yapping for an hour!"

"Indeed, Rasna's mother..."

"Say! a man can do such a thing. It works this way. But a woman? Chhi-chhi. How sinful is..."

A gang of teenage boys shouts from above the tanker that they have found a dog's dropping inside the tanker.

The news creates another layer of chaos that ends with dumping the gallons of water straight onto the road after which the crowd evaporates in a matter of a few seconds.

A Few Days Later

Two women, who were coming from opposite directions, meet at a junction. One is standing on a slightly elevated road and leans down towards the other woman who is lifting her chin to have a closer ear. The first woman looks sorry.

She gasps, " have you heard that ashik's father died yesterday?"

"So I've heard. They say his kidneys were ruined completely by the overconsumption of liquor... Arey, it was bound to happen. He had been complaining of kidney problems for so long. Doctors had advised him not to drink anymore but did he listen..."

"I don't understand what is in that piss after all?"

"God knows...why should we be bothered after all?"

"Who will take care of Ashik's education now? Will his mother's income be enough? It's difficult without a father."

"Indeed. It is what it is. But that witch won't need no husband! She has kept someone for herself. Have you heard of that young boy?"

"I have. Have you noticed the glow on her face? I would have been ashamed if I were her. Not even a fourteen-day has come to an end, but her misery has sure does. There was only one thorn: Her man. It was plucked out alright."

"This is nothing. Remember Sunita? She was worse. After her husband died, her cheeks baked like fresh cookies. And you know what, I had seen her only in ragged clothes but when her husband died she not only began wearing colours of the rainbow every day but the red lipstick on her lips got even brighter too. At least, Ashik's mother was decent enough to show some of her beauty to her husband as well."

"Yeah. Can give her credit for that. Listen didi, I have to go now. My boss's son must be awake by now. I have to cook for him."

"This reminds me of my kids too. I need to make haste. They're going to school."

Both women cross one another and continue walking in opposite directions.

CHAPTER TWO

Eighteen children ranging from three to ten are lined up at different edges of the gully in the companionship of their classmates and secretly of their best friends. Whenever their tuition master notices something suspicious, they immediately move apart pretending they don't even know each other's names but when the master resumes his regular checking, writing, or scolding, they slowly slip near to each other and continue with their endless giggles and whispers. A girl who has a Kohl dot on her forehead and chunky silver anklets on, is snoozing behind her notebook while a boy who is almost behind the master is peeping into the previous pages to ape five birds' names in his test notebook. The master is too busy to notice the smuggling and gambling of erasers and sharpeners that are taking place under his nose. The only concern before him is to encircle the mistakes in the alphabets of two children who are currently standing before him. And while he is busy minding his work, one of the children, standing in front, naughty for sure, is rubbing the blunt tip of the pencil on another's cheek. Utterly unfortunate their time must be, the master notices the mischief this time. He performs two percussions like Zakir Hussain on the naughty child's back. But unlike tabla, the child's body moves along with the flow of the instrumentalist's hands.

Incoming through this pandemonium of the little devils, Jyoti's mother rushes impatiently into Pinky's house. Seeing Pinky's papa sitting inside she drags herself silently towards the other room where she knew that Pinky's mommy would be sewing people's clothes. A tall and seemingly educated woman was standing beside the tailor machine and was talking with Pinky's mother. She goes to straight to the tall lady and whispers to her—

She holds the lady's hand gently, "Did you bring it today?"

"Oh yeah yeah... I was here only because of your work. I handed them over to Pinky's mother. I brought 20 boxes. Is it enough?"

"Enough for now" she shyly giggles. "When an ASHA worker lives so near, why would I bother for numbers of boxes... Arey, sorry for not asking, was it convenient for you?

"Why wouldn't it be! It is sort of my job after all, to take care of the needs of ladies. I take a salary for such services", the tall lady chuckles. "

Leave her! She is obsessed with embarrassment", Pinky's mother laughs. She goes on with exciting fake anger, "...but what I can finally conclude today is that you are truly biased. Jyoti's mother asks for condoms...

"Hushhhhhh...didi... don't say that word so loud!!" Jyoti's mother sinks down in embarrassment and looks behind to check if Pinky's papa is standing nearby. "You will kill me someday with your loud mouth didi", she says.

Pinky's mother suffers the mixed emotions of fun and resisting that fun simultaneously. She laughs silently as she says, "did he hear?"

" I don't think so", says the tall lady. "So, why do you think I'm biased? Tell me now? He is not listening", goes the tall lady.

"Yes... yes... it's because when she asked for that thing, you fulfilled her wish like a Ginnie but I've been asking for pads for a month now and you still haven't got any", says Pinky's mommy who now can hold her laugh.

"Listen didi, I have been trying ever since you asked about it. But you know, it's difficult to get them out secretly. Now, these boxes are not so much in demand so it's easy to steal without suspicion from a huge pile but the sanitary pads vanish like ghosts. Why don't you just come to our center? They won't refuse you know It. It won't take a second."

"Arey, how can I? I don't have time. Look at the mess in that corner. I have to sew all of them within this week. I have so much work. I would have come otherwise."

"Okay didi, i will see what can be done", says the tall lady. She looks at her wristwatch, "Oh it's already nine I have to be there in five minutes. I'm gonna head out now..."

As she goes out, Pinky's mother yells from her place — "if possible, ask for calcium tablets as well". The tall lady replies. Her vanishing voice reverts, "done!".

"Do you still have back pain didi?", asks Jyoti's mother.

"Back pain?", she laughs. "I not only have back pain but added to that, neck pains have also started along."

"You toh, sit for so many hours naa for your work."

"Yeah, it's that. But they say that women's bones melt with age. It could be that. I asked for calcium capsule anyway."

"Achha didi, I'm gonna go now", she says as she barges out of the doorway.

"Oye listen, your things! Won't you take them with you?", asks Pinky's mommy running out behind her.

"No not now", Jyoti's mother comes back to the door from the gully. She goes on in whispers, "It's morning didi, everyone is out. Somebody will notice. It would be embarrassing. Think! For him, it is too embarrassing a thing that he wouldn't even bother to buy one. But I can't afford another child for now and copper T is disturbing. Would you please be kind enough to keep them with you for now..."

"Yes, I can but remember to come back in the evening and take them away".

"Pakka..."

The gully has colourful bubbles like children still floating around. The chaos has still not subsided. The master is dictating and translating sentences from an English textbook and his disciples are repeating after him — "in-the-class-is the- discussion jane is the- you- hardly is the- said- the word- Jane tum bolti nahi class men. Students repeat after them. The master reads next "we is the- all-aired is the- our- opinion- but- from- you is the- we barely heard- hum sab ne kuch bola lekin tun nahi bolti— so children what must we do...?" He asks but students are clueless as ever. So, he explains, "we must discuss things with others...We must have our opinions!". He pauses for a few seconds and yells to a girl, "where have you lost Nargis?!

Everyone is repeating but you! Pay attention!". But apparently Nargis has no idea what master had just dictated so she moves her lips in confusion while other children repeat with the soulless faces, "we must discuss things with others. We can have opinions." The master goes on with the book — " you is the- sat- and- stared is the- in silence...

Both the women are distracted by the children for a few seconds. Diverting attention from the children, Jyoti's mother utters in hesitation, "Listen, didi...do you happen to have a hundred rupees? My kids are not eating vegetables so I was thinking of cooking some samosas for them. But dekho naa, Bedsheet-walah asked for money today and then I spent whatever was left from the daily budget, on flour, oil and paneer. If Jyoti's father comes to know of it, he would shout at me with eyes closed. But I have cleared Bedsheet-wala's debt, I have at least one thing sorted out now."

"When will you return it?" shoots Pinky's mommy.

"Oh, it won't take long I assure you."

"Okay but just wait till I am done with the lining... I can give you some bucks today as Ridhima's mother has promised to take her clothes away by evening. She has 530 left of the four sets of salwar-kurta and a blouse." She explains.

"Her husband is jobless for months now. How do you think she will manage to give you 530?" Inquires Jyoti's mother.

"Don't you know she has found a job at PG in Vilaasniketan. She cooks there. Do you know, she even takes out some food often for her family. This way, she saves money off dinner expenses."

" Listen, I recently came to know something ", she whispers. "I will confide it to you only but first promise me that you won't tell it to anyone."

"Okay. I won't tell. And what do I have for me in it after all? Have you seen me telling such things to anyone?"

"Nah nah...i know you. That's why I am telling you only. You know how bad her condition was. Ashik's mother ran away to God knows where without paying 14'000."

"Eh! I sort of saw that coming. It is not something odd. And say his name properly. It's Ashish. You people have ruined that simpleton kid's name."

"I can say what I can say naa didi. By the way, his mother ran away is a far bigger concern. I take care of the boy now. Let's see when she comes back. Every eloped woman is bound to come back."

"That is why they say women must study. Studious women don't do such things and they can earn for themselves as well."

"Hmm. What you say is right."

"If my parents had taught me I would have found a better job."

"Oh, didi... It's still better than what other women here are doing. They go to paraya people's houses to wash their dishes. At least you do your own business... achha didi I must go now..."

"Arey sit down naa bubba. Talk to me more. What urgent work has fallen?"

"No didi, my children are expecting me. As soon as you lend me a hundred, I will be off."

"Ohho! Wait then. Just giving you. Let me just put your things on that shelf. And don't you forget to take them away by night. Pinky's papa might find them accidentally" says Pinky's mommy as she places the boxes on a shelf in almirah.

She goes on, " achha listen, one more thing. My mother has sent me some khatai to make curries and all. Will you take some?"

"Why not! I have heard so much about your mother's khatai", says the elated voice of Jyoti's mother.

CHAPTER THREE

Nargis is standing on her balcony and staring into the street to see the daily activities. Enveloped in shabby but not too tattered to be tagged as those of beggars clothes. A young woman is wandering in the gullies. She has tugged an infant on the curve of her right hip and with her right hand, she is holding a steel plate on which a few silver coins are shining among a couple of scrambled ten-rupee notes. But she is not all by herself and the baby. A teenage boy who might have just encountered the onset of the youth's spring is showing novel blooms of the moustache below his nose. A layer of dirt is unable to conceal the beaten but still delicate texture of his skin. He is carrying a stick in one hand and the other one is clutching the lady's arm. The lady splutters — "*aye di - di - ji - de - do - na - dekh - lo - na -di - di- mera - ye - bhai - dono - ankho - se - mohtaj - hai - dus - rupiya - di - di- ji- de - do - na...*" (Please give me ten bucks sister, my brother is blind). The shabby lady is dragging her feet lest people will not be able to notice her if she walks swiftly.

"What is this? What've you done to yourself?"

A heavy muffled voice comes from a house nearby situated in a corner. It is Ridhima's– thinks Pinky as she leans on to hear more.

"Who's...who's... dupatta is...is this?" Says the same voice. She thinks Ridhima's parents are fighting again.

A strong voice reverts in the same heavy tone which seems like her mother's, " Why don't you buy me one then? Don't you see I have no good clothes? And which can be called okay, miss one thing or other. I literally had to beg for this one but do you ever understand?" says Ridhima's mommy as she comes out through her doorway.

Grabbing and jerking the dupatta to rip it off, he says, "todayyy...today I will teach you some lessons. You are flying...haan? You're flying since you've started going with those women. Hmm..."

"Nobody teaches me nothing. I have my own brain for your information", she yanks back at him.

Lifting and thrusting it on her back in anger now, "you said what? A brain...oh you have a brain now...you will have to rub your nose at doors to keep this kurta on your body if I die right now...*zaada...zaada bolegi tu?hain?zaada*! You enjoy showing the neighbours that you scold your husband like this. Don't you!...look! Hain? ...tell me!...bol!..."

While saving her face she jumps into the gully now requesting, "Nose...nose...don't hit my nose I said...stop! Will you?"

Her husband looks confused.

She slides the pinch of fingers out over the sides of her nose and finding it naked, she says in a frenzied tone, "Where has it gone?. ..Where is it? ..I lost my nose ring..."

She wipes her hands over the road and shakes her body awkwardly in hope that the nose ring would spring out like a grasshopper. But she gets nothing. She starts to lose her balance and thinking of the gully road as a mother's lap, she dissolves down and says in a damp voice, "I lost a gold earring last time like this..."

And within a glimpse, I can see large drops of tear clutching her lashes "What should I do now? The last blow was hard enough and now you've made me lose this too. How many times did I tell you not to hit my nose!! "

"It's all your fault...all yours!" The husband defends himself by gathering all possible means. He continues in distress, " Why do you do such things that you know can piss me off?"

She can not lose hope this early so she pulls herself together and barges back into the house. She excavates every edge and vertices in one breath. About twenty minutes later, a muffled voice is heard again but the tone is exciting this time. It is she, exclaiming from inside, "I've found it!"

She comes out levitating in excitement and chirps, "what a *budhhu* I'm!...it is right here, you see it? It is right here" she shows the nose ring to her husband which is clasped in the dupatta. She continued holding a giggle trying to find a way to burst out, " I thought I was gone today". The husband keeps his mouth shut and listens with his eyes running haphazardly out of command.

She goes back inside and looks into the mirror fixed adjacent to their main door. "Maybe God knows how tight our conditions are. It is already difficult to save money from medical expenses. I can't afford to lose whatever meagre I am endowed with. Girls are getting bigger every day. We have to save something for them. Don't we?" She says as she wears the nose ring.

By the time the lady-beggar has reached this corner repeating the same words in the same middle note. Ridhima's mommy who wants to return good to god's seemingly good grace grabs a ten-rupee note and flings herself outside. She places the note on the lady-beggar's steel plate and looks towards her man saying,

"Dekho Ji"...pointing finger towards the husband in a firm tone, "you can hit wherever you want, I won't mind but never hit on ears or nose." The husband although looks relaxed at the thought of not losing gold but resists showing any compassion. He answers, "haan...haan...okay."

The husband has left to tend to some work. But Ridhima's mother is still in front of the mirror glancing at herself. She has a graceful look on her face. She closes her eyes and says in a cool releasing breath "Thank you, God! You saved me from a big loss today."

The muffled voices of the begging lady can still be heard saying, "*ye - dono - ankhon - se - andha - hai - aye - di - di..*" Her voice is being buried slowly in the depths of growing layers of gully.

CHAPTER FOUR

Breaking news is flashing across TV screen:

"A family of seven died in Punjab in A SINGLE NIGHT!

Again!!

But what was the cause?

Was it poison?

Was it a serial killer?

Or was it a disaster?

No! None of the above...

But then the question stands: what happened?

How did these SEVEN PEOPLE of one family die IN THE COMFORT of SLEEP? And IN THEIR OWN HOUSE?

But we will tell you! Our channel will tell you!

.

.

.

It was...CARBON MONOXIDE!!!!"

Nargis who is sitting before the news channel feels a sudden bubble of curiosity inside her chest. So she charges into the common room and asks—"what is Carbon monoxide Ammi?" Her parents were relaxing on an archive sofa. They go perplexed at such a random and foreign question. Her ammi says, "how would we know nNshu? We stay illiterate. Why don't you ask your brother? " and they resume their previous activity.

Nargis is a nine-year-old girl who never learned to be at a single place. She is curious about almost everything that her eyes hold. Her elder brother Arsh can often be seen complaining to her mother that Nargis loads him with a shipload of questions— "what is namaaz? And why does Ammi wear a hijab while reading Qur'an? Why is he so tall but not me? Why is the grass green and not yellow? Why doesn't our papa know how to cook although Ammi says it is necessary to learn? Why is potato, a potato?..." and the list is endless. Arsh is a patient young man but when he is busy, it becomes frustrating for him to attend two things at a time. So, Nargis has to be prepared always to bear some shouts and even ear pulling if the time is nowhere near to luck.

After noticing confusing shirks from Abbu and finding Ammi already busy making halaal, she heads straight to the verandah where she believes her elder brother is ready with a Wikipedia in hand. Arsh is sprinkling water on some new saplings and tending to them dearly.

She spits up, " Listen, bhai, what's Carbon Monoxide?"

"What?", Arsh diverts his attention to his little sister with his eyebrows pushing into each other. " What-is-car-bon-mo-no-oxa-eed"

"Oh, Carbon monoxide! It's just a gas bubba. It's poisonous."

"Yeah, so I thought. But tell me more naa...like.. like how it killed them in sleep. Isn't poison supposed to be bitter? Why could they not smell anything different? ", Nargis flashes out.

"Oh, you little lizard! Ask me slowly and who were killed for heaven's sake?" Arsh slaps her gently on the top of her head.

"They are saying on TV that in Punjab, seven members of a family died in their sleep because of carbon monoxide."

"Oh that! Sadly, it happens every winter. See, this gas has more affinity to hemoglobin than oxygen..."

"What!!?"

"How should I tell you in simple words? wait...Yeah! Listen now, our blood loves the company of Oxygen, the gas we breathe but when Carbon monoxide starts to sing mouthfuls of praises to the blood, its love for oxygen diminishes. Gradually, carbon monoxide steals the place of oxygen but can we humans live without oxygen? No, so we die."

"Carbon monoxide is a thief!" Says Nargis wryly. "But why in the winters?"

"It's because in winters many people in the village keep the smoldering coal inside to keep the room warm... and the partially burnt coal is what produces carbon monoxide". Thinking the discussion finished, he turns himself back to his plants.

"But why do people do that? Shouldn't they let windows open a bit?"

"Yes, they must. But unfortunately, many people are not educated enough. Or maybe they are just careless" he says with his back turned to the front again.

"Oh I see...but you still haven't told me why people couldn't find anything different in the air like it's poison. It must have some kind of bad smell? "

"Because, like oxygen, it doesn't have an odor. So in a way, it feels like oxygen. All clear?"

"I think so", she looks doubtful and tries to search for more questions.

"No more questions now, please. I'm done for today. Uncle Imran is coming today to visit us. And look at your dirty clothes... Why do you behave so unruly? Don't you know how to comb your hair? You look like a wild cat."

"Later!" She says quickly and means to hop out of the house but Arsh grabs her gently by the neck and pushes her inside the room. "You won't be going anywhere today," he says with his made-up anger. "Now get yourself into a good frock. The black one with red polka dots would do fine."

"Argh!" Nargis kicks her right foot out in anger.

A Week Later

Nargis's parents are sitting outside after dinner around 11 O'clock. Nargis's Ammi has not been feeling much involved in daily chores. Something does not seem fit to her. So, she decides to share her concern with her husband while the kids have gone to sleep.

"Have you noticed something different in Nargis?"

"No, I don't think so. Have you?"

"Yes, I have. Isn't it why I've been asking you so", she looks more concerned.

"Why? What happened?", Nargis's father too, looks concerned now.

"You men just dive deep into your news and work and reach to another world. Never care to notice something different in this world..."

"Arey, would you please tell me what happened?", Nargis's father bids gently.

"I think something has happened with our Nishu. She remains silent most of the time now. You know how she abhors staying inside. But now, I see stuck to room's corner."

"So you're concerned over such a trivial thing?", says Abbu and laughs. "Maybe it's because she is growing and getting mature like you", he chuckles and touches her cheek with care.

"Arey, don't do it, please. Someone might see us", she tries to push him away. "No, I think something's up."

"And what is that, you think?"

"I don't know. But it could be something related to Imran. You see, on the day Imran left, Nargis came to me. She looked unusually occupied with something. When I asked her what was the matter, she told me that Imran had kissed her."

"But Imran is my cousin. He thinks of her as his daughter. It was nothing but a paternal kiss."

"So what I told her! And I even told her not to mention this to anyone lest people in our neighborhood might use their imagination to paint their own story around a trivial thing such as this. You know how they perceive muslims' customs related to marriages."

"So? What's the matter?"

"I don't know, it doesn't feel fit. I tried to asking more about it but she bailed into her room. I think I would have done something else."

"Like what?"

"No idea"

"Arey don't worry. You handled the matter very well. I'm proud of you.", he caresses her cheeks again. But pulling herself out, she says, "someone WILL see us. But would you understand!", she chimes and heads back into the house behind.

A Week Before

Uncle Imran is a tall man, a little taller than Abbu but his face tells he is way young. Nargis's Ammi is searching for a beautiful and traditional bride for him among family and friends. He looks fair enough but his unproportionately huge hands are what distracts Nargis the most. But she has her own important things to attend to so after bidding salaam to uncle Imran, she storms down into the gully to play with her friends. Uncle Imran is fond of children and if it is a girl, the love is naturally accentuated in his heart. "Khuda ki nemat hai betiyan (girls are gifts from God)", he says to her parents. Nargis is playing hopscotch with Ridhima and Pinky in the gully outside. She looks beautiful today. Arsh's shout was fake though, but it worked well. Red and black do look good on her body which still has not let baby fat go off its embrace.

While Nargis is playing outside, he eagerly watches her from the verandah. The soft and ample body of hers hops with sturdy muscles. Frequent long expeditions outside and all-day play have made her body tight. As she bounces from one box of hopscotch to another, her tightly woven braid bounces up with it and bounces her black frock which has red polka dots. Watching Nargis playing with her friends is like witnessing God himself, he says and gives a bar of delicious melting chocolate to her when she comes back. Nargis can't hold her excitement seeing such a big chunk of chocolate in her hand. She bailes to share it with her friends.

Two Days Ago

Ammi asked Nargis to help her in the kitchen. It is too much of a burden on her with a guest already staying for a week. If it was only family, she would have not made much effort with food but she hesitates to cook simple daal and roti for a guest. Nargis, as usual, has plans; today with

Ridhima, Jyoti and Ashish. They are going to March up to the ruined school behind the garbage dumping spot after school. But since the day Imran uncle arrived, going outside has become a dream. Ammi assigns another work, once she completes one. She feels suffocated. But she really wanted to go to the ruined school today so she asks if Ammi would spare her today. But, would she? Added to that, she scolds hard for even asking. It makes Nargis mad and she runs downstairs and beneath the stairs. She sits beside the new saplings which Arsh had placed to keep them from harsh rays of the sun. Ammi had never shouted so hard at her. It makes her cry even more. She dips her head between the bent knees. Large and warm drops of tears are falling one by one from her eyelashes. She can't think of anything. As she is pouring her anger and sorrow out in liquid, she feels a sluggish and slightly warm thing on her nape. She feels disgusted and lifts her head only to find Imran uncle standing before her. He has a mysterious spark in his eyes and he smiles slyly.

"Ewww... is there something on my nape?". She says as she tries to find something on her nape. Imran uncle keeps on smiling in his sly way.

He says, "Children are meant to be loved naa... your Ammi doesn't appreciate how hard you try. But I do! Poor Nargis... alas! I wish I could be there to take care of you."

"You do? Yeah, I hate her too. She is rude. I will never talk to her again."

"Yeah, me too", giggles Imran uncle.

"But what was it on my neck? I can still feel it!"

"Have you never been kissed? I mean, by your father?", leans Imran uncle to get close to her face.

"Yes, many times... but I like them", she swerves her head away. " Did you just kiss me? It didn't feel like a papa's kiss? It was disgusting", says Nargis wryly.

"You naughty girl!", smiles Imran uncle. His eyes still have that mysterious spark. He goes on, "we must not say such hurtful things to the people who love us". Nargis' eyes are still wet but she is not crying anymore. She is rather curious about Imran uncle's mysterious eyes.

"Now, if you give me a chance I can try to kiss you like your father", he leans more closer to her face as he says. But Nargis has still not recovered from the dirty, wet sensation on her nape and she pulls herself away. Imran uncle tries to calm her down. Her shoulders are grabbed firmly in his huge hands and his eyes are shining evermore. It infuses a distinct fear in Nargis' heart. She gathers all her courage and moves her body heavily to break away from his grip. After a few jerks, she slips herself out. In the haphazard motions of both bodies, he loses his control and falls on his huge hands not before breaking a few new saplings.

CHAPTER FIVE

At 2:49 AM

Imarati is thumping her foot furiously to the floor and hovering her hands in the air, sometimes making fists and sometimes slicing the air with her index finger vigorously in her verandah. Her left hand is holding a mobile close to her ears and she can't stop yelling at the phone. Her man is sitting in a corner on a chair, waiting and looking eagerly at Imarati's face.

Imarati shouts in her balcony—"You...you come right away to me! Come this instant. I have the capacity to keep you in my house and feed you as well...tell your in-laws...you...you..listen first, you don't need to worry. Just leave that rascal's house. We don't need him... what did you say...hmm...yeah...how dare he! Did he really... he said such a thing!? I am telling you just leave him this instant and come to me. I will take care of other things. You just need to pack your bags only. That's the only thing you need to do. I will handle it after that. Do as I say...

...Let that rascal and his bloody family know that we can not only survive without them but are even better... we can live in luxury... What do they think of themselves! Hm?

...Why are you crying beta... it's their time to cry. I will teach them a lesson this time. It's been far too stretched now. What do they think of themselves! Hm?

Okay. Hm...hm..okay ...you just come here and I will be there at the metro station to pick you up."

"Hm...hm...come soon"

"What did she say?", her old man jumps on her with an impatient light in his eyes as soon as she pushes the red button on the mobile keypad.

"How many times have I asked you to bring our daughter back? But could your legs move!...that Dog hit Kajal today. Her In-laws are ordering her to stay at home and take care of the first baby. They are not letting her go back to work", Imarati flashes.

"But why? What is their problem?"

"You know how conservative her mother-in-law is. She says that women in her house never go outside even to buy groceries let alone for work. It is against their pride, they say. My foot! Their rotten pride."

"And what did her man's say in it?"

"It wouldn't be a serious matter if it wasn't for that dog. He just wigs his tail and huffs before her mother. He says yes if his mother says yes and no if she says no."

"Arey, come back to the real matter. Will you..."

They both get inside. Imarati, consumed in thoughts, walks here and there unintentionally. A while later she stops before her old man and splutters — Didn't Kajal tell us about him when we were fixing her with that rascal? He told her that he didn't want anything but only a promise that she would take care of his widow mother. I had my doubts then... A young and ready-to-become-a-groom, should check whether a girl is well educated or if she has a beautiful body and face or not.... what he asks? Nothing but if she will take care of his widow mother. See, I don't mind a child's concern for his mother but one must have his desire too naa... he was about to spend all his rest of life with her after all. Agree or not? He was looking for a wife, not a nurse!"

I agree. I agree. But why did you then let our Kajal marry that bastard?

"I never did. It was our dear Kajal. She was reaching thirty-two. She was worried that people would point fingers at us. More to that, I myself could never bear to hear somebody calling her old. So, I hid her age. When somebody asked I told them that she was only twenty-four. And dekho naa, how many years she lived with us but never did I hear anything unruly and filthy about her behaviour from anyone like they say about Ishita or Ashik's mommy."

"Yeah, I thank God every day for blessing us with such a great daughter."

"But look at her situation now. Despite the years of tapasya, she found a man like that bloody rascal who doesn't even share a single coin from his pathetic salary with her. All that he earns goes straight into that bitch's lap whom he calls Amma. The whole world knows a woman has more needs than mere stomach's!"

"It didn't seem that big of a deal in the beginning though", he says as he begins to recline his chair.

"Our brains were corrupted. I say, why does she need to stay with him now. He couldn't share his salary. It was okay with us. Our daughter was capable enough to get a job? Wasn't she?"

"What you say is right..."

"She didn't ask for money. She bore her expenses. And now they say she can not go out and earn after giving birth to a child."

"But her mother-in-law remains at home. She has sufficient time and energy to take care of the newborn.

Isn't he her first grandson? Every grandma holds affection towards her grandkids."

But she doesn't. You know why? Because she is a ghost. Her feelings are all smoke. They have no weight! She only loves to suck on money. That's all she does. She is a ghost filled with jealousy, greed, hate..."

At this, the old man stands again and asks, "calm down, please. It's past three three and people will soon be waking up. I don't want neighbors to hear about this matter. " He takes Imarati inside and tries to make her rest a bit.

Imarati lowers down her tone along with her body to the bed. Her mouth can be heard uttering gibberish. Her old man fetches her glass of water. She breathes and drinks and calms herself down and then goes again, "they fought with her all night. Our girl did not want us to get worried so she didn't inform us until it went beyond her capacity to bear anymore. You know what that bitch did?"

"What happened?", the old man sits beside her.

"She called over her young brother. You tell me, what was the need after all to call him over? Was he a magistrate or something! Doesn't he have his own household to tend to?"

"So what bubba? Her brother helped her a lot during their money troubles."

"No, the matter is that he doesn't know our daughter's situation. A biased judgement was bound to be made by the bloody dear brother of hers. He took his sister's side naa."

"What did he propose?"

"Like his sister he too ordered Kajal to stay at home and take care of the baby otherwise find another home. He said his sister wouldn't attend to the needs of the baby at all."

"How can she be so rude? She herself has three daughters. Can't she empathize?"

"But her daughters are hoor ki pari and our Kajal is nothing but a beggar before them", says Imarati sarcastically. She goes on, "whenever any of her daughters come, she lifts them onto her head and talks about girl power and shit in volumes but look at how she behaves with her daughter-in-law. Bloody double standards! Her own daughters can wear jeans but if Kajal even dares to touch them, her witchful shrill starts bellowing in the entire house."

"Double standards toh, she has. No doubt. She behaves with us as if we are lowly people only for the reason we are the daughter's parents. She can do it, she has money. We are poor."

"No! I won't have it! Not till I live. I can take care of our daughter and our grandson as well. They need to understand that. Hence, I have told Kajal to come back to us with the baby. She will be here in half an hour... "

Imarati goes before the mirror and manages her dishevelled hair. "Would you please fetch me some decent clothes from almirah?" she asks her old man. He brings the clothes to her and places them on the bed. She goes on, " you must not go with me, you already are not well to be out in the cold. You go to sleep and I will be back in an hour.

At 4:20 AM

A car was moving slowly in the low traffic on the road. A woman was reclining on a seat on the other side of a car. Her naked feet were delicately placed on deck and her face was leaning towards the man sitting beside her. The way she was whispering in his ears it seemed she was smoking the enchanted spells of eternal trap, thought Ishita. Ishita was sitting outside the exit gate of a metro station. She was not anxious like one was waiting for somebody. It was more like a sedated position of some deep meditation as if she was picking a well-defined road in the mash of a complex journey. Imarati was surprised to see Ishita so early in the morning sitting alone outside the metro station. Only a week ago she heard words floating that Ishita had run away with another man and it had been only twelve days since her wedding. She gave a quick forbidding glance to her and turned away to avoid any confrontation. Kajal had said that she was only one station away on the phone. It would hardly take five minutes for her to arrive.

CHAPTER SIX

Like bees stuck to a badge of honey, people have crowded in chauraha. Not unlike bees, they are buzzing in their confusing tamper. Ridhima's mother was returning home from the vegetable market when she saw the whole colony levitating around at one place. Usually such conglomerations indicate either a free feast or a scandal. The chaotic hodgepodge is stringed with all sorts of faces varying from tone, texture, size, and shape to expressions. But among the energetically moving mouth and pairs of eyes, one face is veiled and is staying still in the centre like a confusing piece of art among ignorant spectators.

Ridhima's mommy feels more pumped up with excitement and more curious to find out what after all is the matter. While counting the heads, she finds a familiar face talking to a circle of unknown faces. So, she approaches it and asks, "Listen Didi, what is going around here?"

"To be honest, I have no idea. I have just arrived and I too am asking the same thing", the other replies.

"*Arey, vo nahi thi*, Ishita? She has come back?", said a face which seemed new.

"Returned? As if she had run away or something?"

"Aye lo! Do you even live here? Don't you know what goes on in our area?", said the familiar face.

"Didi, you know how things are so tight at my house. He can't even get a job. I haven't seen a proper salary for about two years so I have to arrange everything from money to bunny. I don't even get time to breathe for two seconds. You tell me then how would I have known all these?"

Looking towards the unknown one, the familiar face says gently, "Poor she, her man is not earning so she has to do everything. She can't be blamed. Can she?"

"Is your husband still not working? How do you manage then, without your husband's earnings? Don't you say anything to him?"

"I tell him everything didi but I can't yell at him he would frown and abuse me instead. I don't want flames of hell up in my house", says Ridhima's mother. Her eyes look as if they want to cry but she stiff her lips and lowers her eyes.

A boy, who must be about four or five, is walking by. He is shouting and laughing in a repeated sequence to the phone he has kept in his right hand. The talking Tom is appearing on his mobile. He shouts, "you whore!!" and the Talking Tom repeats after him in its cartoonized voice. It tickles the boy and he laughs his lungs out and repeats the same word again to hear Tom's funny little echo.

"See , brother of hers. Of course, she doesn't have a blood-brother but her Mausi has two boys. I say, the whole family is spoiled like such. A married sister is running away with her yaar, mother herself had married two times and this little rat is saying such unholy things at such a little age", says the stranger face with her eyes open wide placing a hand on her right cheek.

"Arey didi, he can do away with such things. People won't object but a young girl who is married already is doing such insane things like running away?! What was the benefit after all? Could her yaar keep her?...No, she had to come back naa."

"No, what you are saying is true. Girls nowadays don't measure the consequences of their actions" , says Ridhima's mother. " I too have two daughters. I don't even let them play with gully's boys. This generation should not be trusted a shred."

Driven by passion, aren't all they? Look at this thing in front us! Tell me— will her in-laws welcome her back after this?", says the familiar face that looks concerned.

"Why would he? And you know what her man said to his mother. He was saying, "can she tell me honestly how many men she has slept with after she ran away? I'm not gonna keep her anymore now. You made me marry that whore and now you'll bear her weight not me", exclaimed the unknown face.

"Of course,he is right. Why would he?...Chalo let's assume she slept with only one irrelevant man, but she did indeed. Did her yaar lose his balls after satisfying his thirst for body?"

"Listen, didi" says the unknown, " I toh, have also heard that her yaar was ready to marry her but she stays a bhangi, and he stays a Rajput. The boy's family did not agree on such a sinful marriage? I can't blame them. They only want to keep their house clean."

They remain silent for a while and look at the crowd and then to Ishita who is still standing alone in the center of the crowd with a long veil cast before her face.

"Why is she there alone? What is she waiting for?" Asks Ridhima's mother in confusion.

"The local chief—Satish Chaudhary", says the unknown face. A second later she giggles and says, "he is not coming on purpose you know. The more she stands alone in the crowd, the more miserably she will be ashamed. I say, let her wait for one more hour like this. She'll learn her lesson alright. By the way, he will decide naa whether she will stay with in-laws or her *maa-baap*."

"Arey, what *maa-baap*? Her maa's second husband doesn't earn enough to keep three bodies. So she manages to send a few rupees while she stays at her Mausi's."

"All the same..."

"And her Mausa agrees to keep her and give her food and shelter?" asks Ridhima's mother, still somewhat confused.

"What should I tell you didi, I have heard he doesn't have a good eye on Ishita. People have seen him abusing and even hitting her. I myself saw her once, crying at the doorway."

"Hush! Don't say such things in public. It might ruin her image more", says Ridhima's mother cautiously.

"Ruined?" The unknown face giggles, "ruined is her whole life now. Her Mausi got her married jhatpat to the man who lived down the street in the corner thinking she would be better away from her mausa but see now what she has done with that freedom!"

"I say that this phone-thing has spoiled many girls. They talk all night with god-knows-who and take what they call... silphi... making odd faces to send them later to their yaars. Girls should never be given mobile phones. Ever! ", says the known face.

"What is going to happen with her? Do you have any idea?", asks Ridhima's mother again.

"What will happen? I don't think her in-laws are ever going to accept her. Do you measure? It had been only two weeks of her marriage. I myself would not have accepted her", answers the known face.

"Where will she go then?"

"To hell!! Why should anyone care!", the unknown face yells.

"Arey Didi, don't shout at her. She is naive with such sorts of issues. I just told you how busy she is. She'll know", says the known face and turns towards Ridhima's mother and tells tenderly, "she won't be welcomed back to her in-laws, that is determined and now out of shame, her Mausi too won't be able to keep her. It leaves only one option—her mother's."

"But you say they don't earn enough."

"Yeah, they don't. But that's not our headache. God shows ways to seekers. She will have to earn or something."

Ridhima's mother remains silent. After a minute she says, "let me go and fetch Pinky's mother. Does she know already? I think not. She would have told me if that was the case. Let me go and check what she is still doing after all at home when the entire basti is out here". She briskly diverts into another lane which leads to Pinky's mother's.

The remaining two ladies bring their known-unknown faces to Ishita's veil. Ishita is still standing at the centre of the buzzing mob in chauraha. The black eyes of hers can be seen rolling in a not-so-strange fear and then dissolving at once down in shame beneath her Georgette dupatta.

"Look at the shameful fellow! How is she rolling those potatoes! Arey, only if you had rolled them on your scandalous actions, you wouldn't have to face such a day", says the unknown face and spits intentionally loud to get her attention.

Ishita remains still and dissolved as before at her place, behind the veil staring at her foot. The little brother of hers goes near and asks her to listen to the phone. Out loud he says, "you whore!" and jumps into the puddle of laughter.

CHAPTER SEVEN

A sharp bright coin of sunlight is shuddering on the hard grey floor. It is 11.57 on Sunday evening and Pinky is sitting before her window staring at the dancing curtains swishing up and down in tune with the wind. The curtains are trying to embrace the winds and intending to never let go. But it perhaps is aware that the power to hold a fluid is never a quality that Georgette could brag about. However, she is not in a mood really, to hear attentively the whispers of the curtain. As Pinky is opening her mouth to yawn, she hears the tinkering anklets. It is Ridhima who was getting bored at home alone.

"Where's you mommy?"

"She has gone to chauraha. They were saying Ishita has returned or something. Mommy was shushed about it before me. I saw her going with your mommy to see what they're deciding for Ishita" is Pinky's answer.

"Yeah my mommy didn't tell me much either. I also asked Nargis about it thinking she wandered everywhere. But she had no clue. It's so unlike her. She must have been busy somewhere else. Listen, what are you doing?" asks Ridhima with inquisitive eyes.

"Nothing much...I'm bored. Lights are out. I can't watch Big Boss and it's Sunday!" Says Pinky looking down into the floor.

"Do you know what happened in Big Boss yesterday? Anurag came back through the wild card entry and...he-he the first task that Big Boss gave was to cook ten south indian dishes. And WHAT! They were not supposed to use the Internet.. he he...it was so fun... so fun... I got... mad laughing", Ridhima can hardly speak.

What did you say? I can't even watch it. When *Bhagwan* will bring lights in? I too wanna watch now? ...and and did Anurag win? What did he do? Tell me quickly." Pinky shakes Ridhima by the shoulder in excitement.

"Arey telling you presently. But leave my shoulders first. " Ridhima says worriedly as her shoulders are still being shaked. Pinky frees her and leans to listen carefully.

Ridhima continues, "you know how much he cries about his mother. He wouldn't even touch a roti in the beginning. Would such a person know how to cook? He tried to make Sambar, he was..."

Pinky interrupts, "did he?!!!! Oh I also like Sambhar... we are SO made for each other!", Pinky looks at the ceiling with dreamy eyes as she says. She goes on, "... In fact, mommy has made some TODAY. " She runs towards the kitchen and returns with a bowl filled with Sambhar.

"What!", Ridhima exclaims " you will eat alone?! You know how I die for your house's Sambar?" Cries she.

"Arey, don't worry. Mommy has saved some to give your mother too. You can have some from that which you will, I'm sure" and she chuckles.

"Aye aye captain!... But how did she come to cook Sambar today? You were saying that she hardly listens to your requests."

"God knows but Yes, FINALLY! Never for once at least she does something new at her own will. I had to save my time from studying and help her with chores twice a day to convince her, only then she came to terms with me hmm... I don't get her! You know, she made sambar in—the—very —first—attempt! And it tasted EXACTLY the same as Idli wali aunty sells yet whenever I ask her to cook something new for me, she says, "NO, *Idon'thavetimeforsuchstupidthings!Idon'tknowhowtodoit*! " and blah blah blah blah. She just swirls in her own circle of chores minding her own duties all day long. I guess her world too, unlike this rectangular house, is round. And round she goes from sleeping to cooking to serving to washing to brooming to sewing to bathing to singing to talking to cooking to serving to cleaning to sleeping—swoosh-and-swish-and-swish-and-swash.."

"Swoosh and swish sounds like a washing machine. Oh, Pinky you make me laugh" giggles Ridhima. Both the girls laugh together.

"The work is more, especially on Sundays, obviously, because Papa's day is off, my two brothers and I are also free of school's torture. Thank God for making Sundays yaar! What would've happened to us kids without Sundays? hmm!

...Oshitt I forgot Boodhi Bua. You will freeze after listening to what happened last night." Says Pinky with a sombre face.

"What? What? Tell me naa.."

"So you know how old she is. Must be above hundred. Mommy says that Bua used to be called a witch in her village". She whispers, " she even says that Bua can speak with the ghosts? So, yesterday...throughout the day, she complained that she didn't feel like eating anything and the VERY EVENING she behaved really weird."

"Why ? what did she do?" asks Ridhima in a horrified voice.

"I went down to use the toilet. And there she was, just in front of her cot. Her hair was all untidy and she was making unusual sounds. I went white with fear and without looking anywhere else I rushed back upstairs to my room. I could not sleep the WHOLE NIGHT! hmm... do you know I was sweating like that Halwayi bhaiya underneath the sheets but I couldn't pull it off... I dare not go near her since that day."

"Was it for real?... ohho I will be pissing in my bed tonight. You'll see. I shouldn't have asked you." Pinky pauses for a minute and continues, " tell me anything else I want to divert myself from your Ghost dairies."

"Okay. Hmmm...." She meditates for a while and as light suddenly trapped inside her eyes, she chuckles in excitement, "A funny thing happened today."

"What? ...what?"

" Mommy, as usual, cooked sambar and went straight to bathe. Kittu stormed..."

"Which one? I get confused. Is it your older brother or younger?" Interrupts Ridhima.

"Arey the older is Keenu and Kittu is the younger one. So listen, Kittu stormed inside. The first thing he asks whenever he gets home is ALWAYS, "where's mama!?" and when mommy comes, "gimme food!" She sometimes looks like a servant in some South Indian movie standing in front of her master hiding her both hands inside upper arms. I SSSWEARR never in my life have I seen him taking food by ownself. It is such a simple thing! Go to the kitchen; take a plate; put a couple of rotis; put some sabzi and that's it! I do it every day. And that arrogant rat doesn't eat if mommy doesn't serve. But mommy usually has more work on Sundays. So she was at a new speed today. After doing usual dusting and cleaning she had rushed into the bathroom. So as usual the responsibility automatically had to be transferred to me. Kittu asked for nothing but food so Bua told me to serve him. I refused..."

"Did you really? My brother also doesn't take food by himself. But I can never refuse to serve. Mommy slap me straight and I am back to my corner", Pinky laughs nervously.

"I toh, refused straight away. And why would I do it? Bhagwan has given him too, hands. And when I refuse to do so you know what she says? She says in surprise, "why would he take the food? He's a boy. He doesn't know such janaani-wale things." Ritu ma'am says that women can do everything that a man can but because they have been limited to home affairs only..."

"Ritu ma'am teach you too? " Kavita inquires but Pinky is too absorved to listen. Pinky continues anyways,

"... it is now considered that women are made for housework only. She says it is called a stereotype. She also says that for this reason, we need to study a lot and prove that we can do everything. And we should fight when we are told to do such stereotype-works. So whenever I am told to serve that rat food, I refuse RIGHT AWAY. When mommy asks me to learn to cook and clean, I refuse RIGHT AWAY. Boodhi Bua nags when I don't do my chores. She thinks that I wouldn't survive a day in sasuraal. Only my Papa is modern in this house. He tells me to focus on my studies only so that I can become an officer when I'm an adult. My papa always wanted to do a government job but he was never good at studies you see. But about mommy, I've heard she used to study a lot and she was good at it too. Yet she is constantly attentive that I must learn to do home affairs. She says my husband won't do anything at home. But my papa supports me. He says "of course he will help her!". It makes me giggle every time I think of how I will rule my sasuraal. Mommy won't understand such things. She's not modern I guess, like me or papa."

"It is funny, my Papa says that he wouldn't let me even go to sasural. Papa's are so cool naa.."

"Yeah they are. The other day, papa was resting on the sofa watching TV. My poor papa gets only one day to rest. He does a lot of hard work naa. As he was watching a tollywood movie, he began telling us about his boss. He says that his boss has come straight from hell who likes to torture our petty souls. Oh, how funny he looks when he mimics his boss's orders. He said something like this—"Rakesh ech ech I still haven't got the file! Where ech isit?...Rakesh did you ech email the Budget sheet to Shiv-echech-netram company?!... Rakesh did ech Mishra call back?". People laugh their lives out whenever they are around seeing my papa acting like his stupid boss. He is no less than Kapil Sharma. Do you like Kapil Sharma? I like Kapil Sharma when he makes jokes in Shimona's lips. He once said that she could catch butterflies with such big lips. It was so funny!..."

"Hey, I also watched that episode hmm... her lips are really big. Aren't they? Imagine if you had such lips."

"Hutt!!! go away..." Pinky exclaims. Ridhima laughs at her.

Suddenly Ridhima says, "So what happened with you mommy? Pray, you must come to the main topic now?"

"Oh yes yes...but where was I..?"

"You were saying something like you mommy was busy and she was in toilet..." Ridhima tries to stick pieces together to make sense.

"Arey... not toilet bubba, it was bathroom."

"Eh, same thing."

"yes, yes, I remember now! So When Kittu was asking for food, papa became so angry that mommy was not around. He called mommy a few times loudly asking her to come quickly. I could only hear the muffled voices coming from inside the bathroom. I was looking at his hands. He was grabbing the TV remote in a tight fist while yelling from the sofa. After a while, he called Kittu near and stroked his head, and told him, "mommy is coming beta but until then you can watch TV with me. Hm? ". I don't know what happened but something didn't feel right to me. So I slowly rose up and went to the kitchen to scoop some delicious sambar out and gave it to him so that no one had to yell now. And one serve can not turn into a habit after all. Isn't it? What could I do? Mommy was not there, SOMEBODY had to do it naa! So I did it! It is my family after all. So as I was pouring another bowl of sambar for Kittu when I heard the bathroom door opening. In a fraction of a second mommy entered. She hurriedly said, "doing it right away, just give me a second..." Then she paused and looked at me and said, "Oh Rashhu is doing it already? arey waah! Keep it up beta!".

Pinky continues her story and says, " You wouldn't BELIEEEVE her saree was hanging -looseALL OVER the floor. She was saying something like " *ifthoughtkittuwouldgoemptystomach...didn'tevenrubsoap*

...couldn'tfindtimetotiethesaree" this and that while HERE I WAS- laughing- my stomach out at her silly look. Bhagwan! I didn't care for her compliment I swear!"

"Hwww, is it true? I would have melted into water in embarrassment if I were her. Yet I wish I had such a house..." Both girls laugh hysterically.

Pinky stirs the soup and puts it down on the table to rest. As she resumes her chat with Ridhima in a faint noise, the liquidy lentils of sambar in the bowl are moving like a tornado. They give the loose spoon a jerk after every few seconds. The shreds of tomato, potato, pumpkin, beans, brinjal, are cycling along, and gradually coming to the center with the weakening heat. With the decreasing number of jerks now the tornado's eye is also closing. The spoon too will come to stand-still when it is time.

Putul Mangni Mandal

Living in New Delhi, Putul Mangni Mandal was born in December 1996. It is a pseudonym that she has adopted for the literary world. By root, her family comes from Bihar and as mentioned in the name, she belongs to the Mandal community. However, she abhors rigid statism or communism. Putul (meaning doll is her mother's pet name) lives with her small family of four. Financially, she is lower middle class. She studied in a government school named Sarvodaya Co. Ed. Senior Secondary in Nanak Pura. She has done her Post Graduation in English from Delhi University and aspires to become a professional writer, too, among many other possible-impossible things.

Poems have fascinated her ever since she read *Kanyadān*, a poem by the famous romantic Hindi writer Suryakānt Tripāthi 'Nirālā' in tenth grade. But she never knew that she could write until the day when her teacher Minākshi Mehta asked the whole class to create something. She composed her first poem *Lakshya*. Since then she wrote many poems for her family, friends and teachers. But these poems did not necessarily resonate with her. She thought poems were nothing but a set of stanzas with a particular rhyme scheme. Due to her busy studious life, her writing shrank to zero. But then again about five years later when she was enrolled for Post Graduation in Literature, the withered skills received its second set of monsoon and she began writing poems again. This time it was different. During Post Graduation, even way before reading Wordsworth, she had realised that poems were not limited to mere fancy words and melodious tempo. One day, half asleep, she thought she heard 'Alākh Niranjana' but when she came back to her senses, she found it was actually an evening 'azān' coming from a mosque nearby. It was such a mesmerizing experience that she transformed it into her first English poem *Dream?*. That day she realised how few words, assembled in a way, distorted, twisted, expanded, or repeated could contain an ocean of meaning. She finally met what an honest poet would call — a poem, that day. Some of her English poems include *Once On a Bus, Chores, Substitute, Nowadays, At Last, A Signal of Hope* and many others. She also writes in Hindi/Urdu and some of them are *Intezār, Ūpar-Neechey, Bheetar, Chāl* etc. Fingers crossed, she hopes to soon come up with her poem collection.

Expanding the horizon of possibilities, she has initiated writing short stories as well. To be honest, she needs to work more in that area to come up with one of them publicly. But this novella titled *Listen Didi* is her first official work in prose writing. Being an introvert, most of her days are spent in a corner at home writing, reading, studying or sketching. She has to attend to some chores as well. unfortunately. Hence, she mostly writes from her limited personal experience. Living in a slum area herself, Putul was noticing many small incidents happening in her gully. Insignificant they might have seemed to almost everyone due to their repetition, she decided to use them and create simple stories around them. When her friend and mentor Swarnika asked her to create a work, she decided to give it a try and thus, *Listen Didi* emerged. She hopes that people will find something interesting and unique in her work.

9 798885 558266

Printed by Libri Plureos GmbH in Hamburg, Germany